sadiegardnerbooks@gmail.com
FIRST EDITION
www.sadiegardnerbooks.com

This book belongs to

....

....

Mike had a pet monkey named Monty,
the monkey was really quite smart.
Everywhere Mike went Monty followed,
they didn't like to spend time apart.

Mike can be timid when making new friends,
but his pet monkey had a good plan.
Monty pulled faces and said, "Be yourself,"
Mike smiled and thought, "Yes, I can!"

Mike was racing his sister in the park,
he could never win no matter how fast he ran,
but when Monty shouted, "You can do it!"
Mike ran and said, "Yes, I can!"

"Yes, I Can!"

Mike was scared of trying new things,
when riding his bike he needed a hand,
but when Monty was there encouraging him,
he rode and said,

It was Mike's first day in his new class at school.
His new teacher was a very nice man.

When Mike got shy he thought about Monty.

He then said to himself,

It was Mike's turn to do the chores,
he had to take the rubbish to the trash can.
"The bag is too heavy! I can't do it", Mike shouted,
but then Monty said,
"You are strong, yes you can!"

"I can't wash the dishes!" Mike told his mom,
"I'll drop a dish or a pan."

Then the monkey washed three plates without dropping one
"If Monty is helping, yes, I can!"

It was Mike's turn to read in front of the class,
"I don't want to," he cried. "Why can't Dan!?"
Monty took the book and sat on Mike's knee,
so with confidence, Mike said,
"Yes, I Can!"

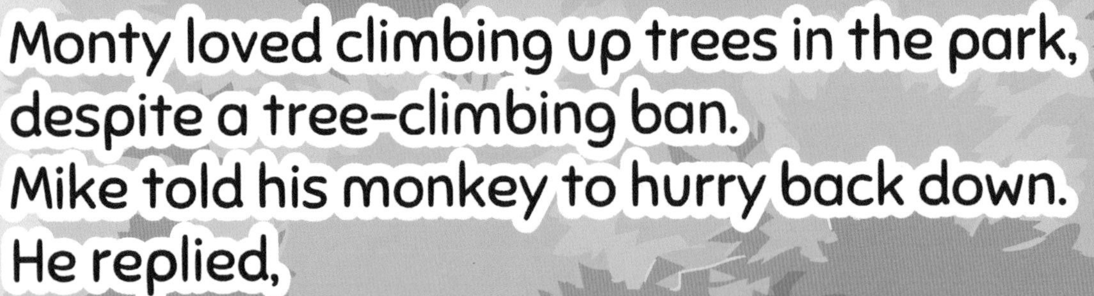

Monty loved climbing up trees in the park,
despite a tree-climbing ban.
Mike told his monkey to hurry back down.
He replied,

"Can a monkey climb trees? Yes, I can!"

Mike had to reach Monty to make him come down,
getting stuck halfway wasn't his plan.
He was nervous, but Monty waved down from above,
"Be brave, Mike, you can make it."

"Yes, I Can!"

You need to be confident in all that you do,
just do the best that you can.

You will not succeed if you don't even try,
be like Mike and his monkey, say,
"Yes, I Can!"

THE END

THANK YOU

I read and appreciate your feedback and reviews. It would mean the worlc to me if you would leave a review on Amazon – this would help support me to create more children's books!

Simply open up your camera on your smart phone, hover over the QR code and click the banner that appears to leave a review!

About the Author

Sadie Gardner is a children's book author from London. She prides herself on creating stories with valuable lessons and messages within them.

Follow me on

Instagram: Sadiegardnerbooks

Facebook: fb.me/sadiegardnerbooks

Twitter: twitter.com/SadieGardbooks

Be notified when my next book gets released, and get it at a discount!

Or Visit
tinyurl.com/y43zh2ft

Simply scan the QR code, enter in your email address, and I will notify you when my next 'Mike and His Pet Monkey' book has been released, further to this, you will get it at a discounted rate!

Collect more books from the 'Mike And His Pet Monkey' Series!

Or Visit
tinyurl.com/y4ukovqh

Printed in Great Britain
by Amazon